THE GREATEST ADVENTURES IN THE WORLD

GULLIVER
IN
LILLIPUT

TONY BRADMAN & TONY ROSS

ORCHARD BOOKS

ORCHARD BOOKS
338 Euston Road, London NW1 3BH
Orchard Books Australia
Level 17/207 Kent Street, Sydney, NSW 2000
ISBN 978 1 40830 575 1 (hardback)
ISBN 978 1 40830 576 8 (paperback)
The text was first published in Great Britain in the form of a gift collection called
Heroes and Villains with full colour illustrations by Tony Ross, in 2008
This edition first published in hardback in 2010
First paperback publication in 2011
Text © Tony Bradman 2008
Illustrations © Tony Ross 2010
The rights of Tony Bradman to be identified as the author and of Tony Ross to be
identified as the illustrator of this work have been asserted by them in accordance
with the Copyright, Designs and Patents Act, 1988.
A CIP catalogue record for this book is available from the British Library.
1 3 5 7 9 10 8 6 4 2 (hardback)
1 3 5 7 9 10 8 6 4 2 (paperback)
Printed & bound in the UK by J F Print Ltd., Sparkford, Somerset.
Orchard Books is a division of Hachette Children's Books,
an Hachette UK company.
www.hachette.co.uk

CONTENTS

CONTENTS

CHAPTER ONE

THE LITTLE PEOPLE

GULLIVER WAS A MAN WHO liked to travel. It wasn't just that he enjoyed visiting distant, exotic places. What he loved most was meeting new people, and learning as much as he could

about them. He went on many voyages, and saw many strange and wonderful things. And this is the story of his visit to the strangest, most incredible country of all.

The voyage started well enough. Gulliver and his fellow explorers headed for the South Seas, stopping to study plants or people wherever the fancy took them.

Then one night their vessel ran into a storm and began to sink. But most of the crew were swept overboard while they were still trying to launch the lifeboat.

Soon Gulliver found himself alone in the sea, desperately struggling to keep his head above the water, until finally darkness swept over him…

He was woken by the warm sun on his
face, and the lazy sound of surf hissing
over a reef. He had survived! He realised
the sea had dumped him on a beach – and
that he couldn't stand up. When he
looked down, he saw he must have been
tied down while he was asleep. Dozens
of fine strings attached to tiny pegs in
the sand criss-crossed his whole body.

Gulliver raised his head…and to his astonishment, he saw a tiny person standing on his chest looking back at him. The little man was no taller than a toy soldier, and was holding a miniature bow and arrow in his tiny hands. Gulliver felt a tickle of movement on his legs and body and, before long, the little archer was joined by a dozen more like him.

"I must be going mad…" Gulliver murmured at last. Then he yelled, "Get off me!" and the little archers screamed and ran for their lives.

Gulliver strained against his bonds and managed to free his arms. He instantly heard a soft whooshing noise and realised that the little archers were shooting at him. Their tiny arrows prickled into his hands and face like a host of wasp stings. The pain told him he wasn't mad, and that what was happening was all too real.

He saw now that there were hundreds of tiny people on the beach. The little archers were firing steadily at him, but the rest were fleeing in panic, screaming at the tops of their tiny voices. Suddenly Gulliver understood. To them he was a giant, so it was hardly surprising they thought he might be a threat. How could they know he wouldn't hurt anyone, big or small?

It also occurred
to Gulliver that
this was a fantastic
opportunity for
him to learn. He
had never
encountered anything like these little

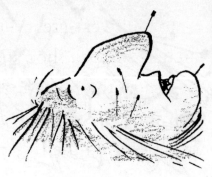

people, and he had so much to ask them.
Then a tiny arrow landed right on the end
of his nose, and he realised he would have
to make friends with them first.

"OK, you win!" he said, smiling.
"I promise I won't hurt you." Then he
put his arms down – making quite sure
there were no tiny people under them
to be crushed – and lay still. "Oh yes,
I er…surrender," he added.

To Gulliver's great relief, the little archers stopped shooting, and the others overcame their fear and started to return. Within a few minutes, the beach was full of activity, all the tiny people hustling and bustling around him.

They built a big trolley, winched Gulliver onto it, then harnessed dozens of tiny horses to one end. Soon he was being carried through a countryside of tiny hills and streams, tiny trees and hedges, and tiny fields with tiny cattle and sheep.

There were even tiny villages full of

tiny people who came out to gawp.
Gulliver gawped back, enthralled.

At last the trolley creaked to a halt,
and there before Gulliver was an amazing
sight – a perfect little city surrounded by
a wall, the battlements full of tiny people
yelling with excitement.

Gulliver was winched off the trolley
and his bonds were removed – although
not before one of his ankles was chained
to a large rock some distance from the
city's gates.

After a while, a column of tiny horsemen cantered out, all of them wearing shiny breastplates and helmets with nodding plumes. They formed two ranks facing each other, raised tiny trumpets and blew a fanfare. Then a tiny coach drawn by four tiny white horses emerged from the gateway and came to a halt. Two tiny footmen ran up to open the door, and a tiny man climbed out.

He was wearing a tiny golden crown, lavish clothes and fancy shoes with rather high heels.

He had a little round tummy, short skinny legs and a snooty expression on his face.

Gulliver immediately guessed this was someone important, although he couldn't help noticing the little man was very small, even for an inhabitant of this country of tiny people.

CHAPTER TWO

THE EMPEROR OF LILLIPUT

THE CROWD ON THE battlements cheered and clapped, and the little man waved vaguely in their direction. Then he turned to Gulliver, and spoke.

"I trust you are ready to humbly beg my forgiveness for your arrival on the shores of my empire," he said. "I don't remember giving permission for anyone like you to visit us. In fact, who – or rather, what – are you?"

"My name is Gulliver, and I suppose I'm, er…a human being," our hero replied. "My ship went down in a storm and I was washed up on your beach. I really am terribly sorry if I've caused you any trouble…"

"A human being?" scoffed the little man. "That's utterly ridiculous. We are proper-sized human beings, while you are obviously a giant.

And as for your name – well, I couldn't possibly say anything so barbarous. I shall call you the Great Man-Mountain."

The crowd burst into cheering and applause again, and the little man gave them another vague wave. "Right, er…that's fine," said Gulliver, trying to be friendly. "And would you mind telling me who you are?"

"Me? I am the Emperor of Lilliput, of course," the little man spluttered crossly, "Lord of All I Survey, High and Mighty Ruler, Conqueror of…"

"Ah, so your country is called Lilliput," said Gulliver, leaning forward eagerly. "How fascinating! There's just so much I want to ask you – the kind of food you eat, the houses you live in. Your history, your gods… I want to know absolutely everything."

"I'm afraid that all sounds very boring," said the emperor, and there was a murmur of agreement from the crowd. "In any case, I haven't got time to answer a lot of stupid questions."

"Please, hang on a minute, er…Your Majesty," said Gulliver, feeling slightly irritated. But he told himself to relax and stay calm. He would have to try harder…and keep his patience. "I'm not a boring person, er…I mean giant," he said, smiling. "Honestly, I can be lots of fun when you get to know me."

"Is that so?" said the emperor. "A spot of fun would be good.

Well, don't just sit there, Man-Mountain.
Show me what you can do."

"Right," said Gulliver, "Well, does
anyone want a thrilling ride?"

Many of the tiny people backed off, but
plenty eagerly stepped forward, and
Gulliver allowed three
to climb onto his
palm. Then he
swung them in a
high, graceful arc
through the air,
and over to where
the emperor was
standing. They jumped off,
screaming with excitement and pleasure
and calling out to their friends.

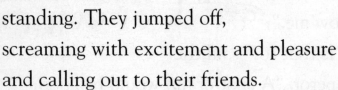

"That looks good, Man-Mountain," said the emperor, smiling up at him. "I am therefore happy to grant you leave to stay in my empire for the time being, and to be in my service. Now I should like a ride myself."

"Why, of course, Your Majesty," said Gulliver. "Climb aboard."

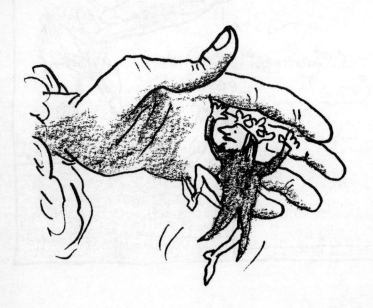

CHAPTER THREE

THE GREAT MAN-MOUNTAIN

AND SO BEGAN A STRANGE time for Gulliver. The Great Man-Mountain provided the emperor and people of Lilliput with lots of entertainment. He gave thrilling rides to hundreds of Lilliputians. He sat still while he let hundreds more clamber over him.

After a while, he tried asking the tiny people questions, but they were always too busy enjoying themselves to give him any proper answers.

The emperor liked Gulliver to put him in the top pocket of his jacket, and to stand up so that he could survey his empire from a great height. "Er...I was wondering if I could ask a favour, Your Majesty," Gulliver said one day.

The emperor was in his top pocket, peering through a telescope. "Ask away, Man-Mountain. Feel free."

"That's just it, Your Majesty," said Gulliver. "I don't feel free at all, and I'd like to. Is there any chance you could have me…unchained?"

"Oh no, definitely not," said the emperor, scowling. "I can't have you blundering about causing havoc with those giant feet of yours!

Besides, I want you here, ready to entertain me whenever I desire it. Considering what it's costing me to keep you fed, it really is the least you can do."

Gulliver scowled now too.

Three times a day, at breakfast, lunch and dinner, a procession of little wagons brought him food and drink. Gulliver always ate everything, and at first he had felt guilty. The emperor had told him he

got through the same amount in a day as the average Lilliputian family consumed in ten years. But the emperor had said it *so* many times, Gulliver's guilt had at last turned into irritation. He couldn't help having a big appetite, could he? After all, he was a giant!

"Well then, Your Majesty," Gulliver said grumpily, "have you seen enough for today? Or are there any other services I can perform for you?"

"Not that I can think of at the moment," said the emperor. "But I…"

"Good," said Gulliver, plucking the emperor from his pocket and returning him to the ground. "See you tomorrow…worse luck," he muttered under his breath. Then he sat down with his back to the emperor and the city.

He brooded for ages, hardly even feeling the crowd of Lilliputians swarming all over him.

Gulliver had been in Lilliput for several weeks now, and he knew no more about it than the day he had arrived. He didn't even know if there had been any other survivors from his ship, or how he would eventually get home.

The next day, the emperor arrived as usual for his time with the Great Man-Mountain. But just as he was about to put the emperor in his pocket, a tiny horseman came cantering up.

"Your Majesty, I bring evil tidings!" the messenger said, his voice trembling. "The King of Blefuscu has declared war on us. He's gathered a great invasion fleet, and it looks like he will attack us…today!"

CHAPTER FOUR

A HOST OF LITTLE SHIPS

THE EMPEROR WENT PALE AND
shouted at his officials, who ran
around in total panic. Gulliver assumed
that Blefuscu was a neighbouring country
– and he realised that this might be his

chance to get what he wanted.

"Excuse me, Your Majesty," he said. "Perhaps I can help? I gather these Blefuscans are the same size as you Lilliputians," said Gulliver. "So don't you think that a Great Man-Mountain could very easily sort them out for you?"

"Why, of course…" said the emperor. He began to smile. "You may have your uses after all,

Man-Mountain. Unchain
the giant, you men!"

"Wait a second,"
said Gulliver. "I'll
only help on two
conditions: you
have to promise
not to keep me
chained up when I
return, and to answer
all my questions. Is it a deal?"

"Yes, yes, whatever…" muttered the
emperor, frowning and vaguely waving his
hand. "Just get on with it, will you? And
don't take all day!"

"OK, keep your hair on," muttered
Gulliver. "Where do I have to go?"

The emperor and his subjects all
pointed in a particular direction, and
Gulliver set off, their cheering ringing

in his ears. Soon he
came to a sandy
beach. And there,
on the other side of a
narrow channel,
was Blefuscu.

Gulliver took off his jacket
and shoes and waded into
the sea.

Gulliver arrived to find
a host of tiny ships in a
little harbour. He took hold
of all their anchor chains,
tying them together and pulling

the whole lot out behind him. Of course, the Blefuscans were terrified, and most of them screamed and leaped into the sea.

The sea was cold, the current strong, and in the middle of the channel it even pulled Gulliver off his feet. He struggled for a while, and glimpsed an island in the distance, beyond Blefuscu...then his feet touched sand again, and he turned towards Lilliput. He left the Blefuscan ships bobbing offshore and crawled up the beach, relieved to be on dry land at last.

"Well done, Man-Mountain!" said a voice. Gulliver looked up and saw the emperor standing nearby. "Now I want you to bring those ships in a little closer so we can start getting my army aboard. We'll soon show those Blefuscans a thing or two, especially with you leading the invasion."

"Oh no, I'm not doing that," Gulliver replied. "What do you think I am? I might be a giant to you, but I'm not an ogre.

Besides, we've got a deal. I stop
the invasion, and you answer all my
questions – remember?"

"Who cares about your
stupid questions?" hissed
the emperor. "You are my
servant, Man-Mountain,
and you will obey my
orders instantly."

"Right, that's it," said
Gulliver, his patience snapping. "I can see
I'm not going to find out anything while
I'm here, and frankly I don't really care
any more. I'd like to say I've enjoyed my
stay in your country, Your Majesty, but
I haven't, not one little bit. And now
I'm off. Cheerio!"

Gulliver waded into the water and
gathered the fleet's anchor chains once
more. "Stop!" the emperor squeaked.
"I utterly forbid you to leave!"

But Gulliver took no notice. He headed
out to sea, and towards the island he had
glimpsed beyond Blefuscu, pulling the
Blefuscan ships behind him.

Anywhere would be better than Lilliput, he thought, even if it was a desert island. Although, as he discovered, he couldn't have chosen a better place. For when he arrived, he found the lifeboat from his ship washed up on the beach!

Soon Gulliver was sailing for home, with enough food and water from the Blefuscan fleet's supplies to keep him going for days. He gripped the tiller as a breeze filled the lifeboat's single sail, a little fed up that his stay in Lilliput seemed to have been such a waste of time.

Then he smiled, realising that he had learned several things after all.

Gulliver knew now that people of any size could be unpleasant and vain – and also that he might not be quite as patient as he had always thought. Mind you, he couldn't wait to start planning a new voyage…

GULLIVER IN LILLIPUT
People Who Behave Badly

By Tony Bradman

The story of Gulliver has always been hugely popular. Like *Robinson Crusoe*, that other famous tale of a traveller, it hasn't been out of print since it first appeared, in 1726. There have been countless film versions, it's been translated into many languages, and most people encounter the story at some stage.

Its author, Jonathan Swift, didn't write it as a children's story. He was born in 1667 and died in 1745, living through a time of great change in Britain and Ireland. He worked as a secretary and spent many years as dean of St Patrick's in Dublin. And he wrote books on all kinds of subjects.

Most of them were what we call satires – in his books he poked fun at the stupid things people said and did. *Gulliver's Travels* is full of jokes about the people and events of that time. For instance, in the character of the Emperor of Lilliput, Jonathan was mocking George the First, Britain's unpopular king.

That was long ago, though, and most of the things Jonathan was writing about have been forgotten. So why are we still fascinated by Gulliver? Partly because the story is packed with exciting events and interesting characters. The voyage to Lilliput is only the first part of the original book. In the other parts, Gulliver visits a land of giants, a flying island, and a country where horses rule.

There's more to Gulliver's lasting appeal, though. Wherever Gulliver goes he meets people, and he studies what they do and say. He discovers it doesn't matter whether they're tiny or enormous, they all behave in certain ways. Some are friendly, but a lot of them are not, and Gulliver tries to find out why.

And in the end, there's simply something deeply fascinating about the contrasts in the story. The image of the giant Gulliver pinned down by those tiny people sticks in the minds of readers – and will continue to do so for a long time to come.

ORCHARD MYTHS AND CLASSICS

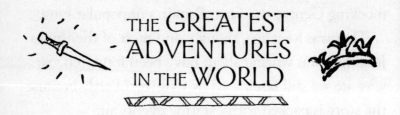

THE GREATEST ADVENTURES IN THE WORLD

TONY BRADMAN & TONY ROSS

All priced at £8.99

Orchard books are available from all good bookshops,
or can be ordered from our website: www.orchardbooks.co.uk,
or telephone 01235 827702, or fax 01235 827703

Prices and availability are subject to change.